This
Treasure Cove Story
belongs to

THREE LITTLE PIGS

A CENTUM BOOK 978-1-912396-19-1
Published in Great Britain by Centum Books Ltd.
This edition published 2018.

3 5 7 9 10 8 6 4 2

Centum Books Ltd, 20 Devon Square, Newton Abbot,
Devon, TQ12 2HR, UK.

www.centumbooksltd.co.uk | books@centumbooksltd.co.uk
CENTUM BOOKS Limited Reg.No. 07641486.

A CIP catalogue record for this book is available
from the British Library.

Printed in China.

centum

WALT DISNEY'S THREE LITTLE PIGS

Illustrations by the Walt Disney Studio
Adapted by Milt Banta and Al Dempster
from the Walt Disney Motion Picture 'The Three Little Pigs'

nce upon a time there were three little pigs who went out into the big world to build their homes and seek their fortunes.

The first little pig did not like to work at all. He quickly built himself a house of straw.

Then off he danced down the road, to
see how his brothers were getting along.
And as he danced he sang:

'I built my house of straw,
I built my house of hay.
I toot my flute,
I don't give a hoot,
And play around all day.'

The second little pig was building himself a house, too. He did not like to work any better than his brother, so he had decided to build a quick and easy house of sticks.

Soon it was finished, too. It was not a very strong little house, but at least the work was done. Now the second little pig was free to do what he liked.

What he liked to do was to play his fiddle and dance. So while the first little pig tooted his flute, the second little pig sawed away on his fiddle, dancing as he played.

And as he danced he sang:

'I built my house of sticks,
I built my house of twigs.
With a hey diddle-diddle
I play on my fiddle,
And dance all kinds of jigs.'

Then off danced the two little pigs down the road together to see how their brother was getting along.

The third little pig was a serious little pig. He was building a house, too, but he was building his with bricks. He did not mind hard work. He wanted a strong little house, for he knew that in the woods nearby there lived a big bad wolf who liked nothing better than to catch little pigs and eat them up!

Slap, slosh, slap! Away he worked, laying bricks and smoothing mortar between them.

'Ha-ha-ha!' laughed the first little pig,
when he saw his brother hard at work.

'Ho-ho-ho!' laughed the second little pig.
'Come down and play with us!' he called.

But the busy little pig did not pause.
Slap, slosh, slap went the bricks on mortar
as he called down to them...

'I build my house of stones.
I build my house of bricks.
I have no chance
To sing and dance,
For work and play don't mix.'

'Ho-ho-ho! Ha-ha-ha!' laughed the two lazy
little pigs, dancing along to the tune of the
fiddle and the flute.

'You can laugh and dance and sing,'
their busy brother called after them, 'but
I'll be safe, and you'll be sorry when the
wolf comes to the door!'

'Ha-ha-ha! Ho-ho-ho!' laughed the two little pigs again and they disappeared into the woods singing a merry tune...

'Who's afraid of the big bad wolf,
The big bad wolf, the big bad wolf?
Who's afraid of the big bad wolf?
Tra-la-la-la-la-a-a-a!'

Just as the first pig reached his door,
out of the woods popped the big bad wolf!
The little pig squealed with fright and
slammed the door.
'Little pig, little pig, let me come in!'
cried the wolf.
'Not by the hair of my chinny-chin-chin!'
said the little pig.

'Then I'll huff, and I'll puff, and I'll blow your house in!' roared the wolf.

And he did. He blew the little straw house to pieces!

Away raced the little pig to his brother's house of sticks. No sooner was he in the door, when knock, knock, knock! There was the big bad wolf!

But of course, the little pigs would not let him come in.

'I'll fool those little pigs,' chuckled the big bad wolf to himself. Then he said out loud, 'Those little pigs are too smart for me. I'm going home.'

He started off toward the deep woods, but he did not go far. He hid behind a big tree.

Soon the door opened and the two
little pigs peeked out. There was no wolf
in sight.

'Ha-ha-ha! Ho-ho-ho!' laughed the two
little pigs. 'We fooled him.'

Then they danced around the room,
singing happily...

'Who's afraid of the big bad wolf,
The big bad wolf, the big bad wolf?
Who's afraid of the big bad wolf?
Tra-la-la-la-la-a-a-a!'

Soon there came another knock at the door. It was the big bad wolf again, but he had covered himself with a sheepskin, and was curled up in a big basket, looking like a little lamb.

'Who's there?' called the second little pig.

'I'm a poor little sheep, with no place to sleep. Please open the door and let me in,' said the big bad wolf in a sweet little voice.

The little pig peeked through a crack of the door, and he could see the wolf's big black paws and large sharp fangs.

'Not by the hair of my chinny-chin-chin!'

'You can't fool us with that sheepskin!' said
the second little pig.

'Then I'll huff, and I'll puff, and I'll
blow your house in!' cried the angry
old wolf.

So he huffed,
    and he PUFFED,
        and he *puffed*,
            and he HUFFED,
and he blew the little twig house
to pieces!

Away raced the two little pigs, straight
to the third little pig's house of bricks.

'Don't worry,' said the third little pig
to his two frightened little brothers.
'You are safe here.' Soon they were all
singing happily.

This made the big bad wolf perfectly
furious!

'Now by the hair of my chinny-chin-chin,'
he roared, 'I'll huff, and I'll puff, and I'll blow
your house in!'

So the big bad wolf huffed and he PUFFED,
and he *puffed* and he HUFFED, but he could
not blow down that little house of bricks!
How could he get in? At last he thought
of the chimney!

So up he climbed, quietly. Then with
a snarl, down he jumped – right into a large
tub of boiling water!

With a yelp of pain he sprang straight up the chimney again and raced away from the little house as fast as he could go!

The three little pigs spent their time in the strong little brick house singing and dancing merrily. And the big bad wolf never came back again.

Treasure Cove Stories

Book list may be subject to change.